# Little Pugs
# Love the Tub

## by Liza Charlesworth

ISBN: 978-1-338-78285-1
Illustrated by Kevin Zimmer
Copyright © 2021 by Liza Charlesworth. All rights reserved.
Published by Scholastic Inc., 557 Broadway, New York, NY 10012.

10 9 8 7 6 5 4 3 2 1    68    21 22 23 24 25 26 27/0

Printed in Jiaxing, China. First printing, June 2021.

Little pugs love the tub!
**Each** pug has a duck.

Little pugs love the tub!
**Each** pug has a boat.

3

Little pugs love the tub!
**Each** pug has a fish.

Little pugs love the tub!
**Each** pug has a book.

Little pugs love the tub!
**Each** pug has a bone.

Mama pug pulls the plug!

**Each** pug has a hug.